# Sam's Big Cookout!

**Written and Illustrated
by Mr. ChickenBiscuits**

Discover more Sam books, free coloring pages, puzzles, and so much more!  Please visit:

**MrChickenBiscuits.com**

Sam's Big Cookout!
by Mr. ChickenBiscuits
Sam the Dog Book Series, Book 4
ISBN: 9781790482917 (paperback)
ASIN: B07L8L3L9S (Kindle eBook)
Publisher: Mr. ChickenBiscuits Enterprises
Murfreesboro, Tennessee, USA

Sam woke up early. Today was Saturday—the fourth of July. It was a *special* day. Today was the day of Sam's big cookout!

Sam was thinking about hamburgers. Burgers were Sam's favorite. Sam could almost taste those burgers now.

There were so many things to do! Sam got started right away. First, Sam set up the grill.

Next Sam went to the kitchen and washed his paws in the sink.

Then Sam got his baseball hat from the closet.
And his special apron. It was a very special
apron. After all, this was a very special day!

Sam wanted everything to be perfect. Let's see... Plates. Forks. Sam even had a long flipper to turn the burgers while they cooked.

Sam was thinking about the other things he needed for his cookout. Just then, a cat ran across the yard!

"Meow," purred the cat.
"Grrrr," growled Sam.
Then Sam chased that cat away!

"Hmmm. Now, where was I?" thought Sam.
Then Sam remembered. He was thinking
about what else he needed for his big cookout.

Sam had no charcoal for the grill! So, Sam went to the store to buy some.

While Sam was at the store, Sam saw potato chips. Sam loved potato chips. So, he got those too. Then Sam rushed back home to start his big cookout!

Sam poured the charcoal into the grill. But wait! Sam had no matches to start the fire!

No matches?  Well, there was only one thing
Sam could do:  go back to the store.  When
he got there, Sam saw cookies.  Sam loved
cookies.

So, Sam got cookies too.  Then Sam raced back home again to start his big cookout!

Now Sam had everything: plates, forks, charcoal, matches, potato chips and cookies. Now what? Sam had nothing to drink! Oh, well, back to the store...

This time Sam saw candy at the store. Sam loved candy. So, Sam got some candy too. And bananas. And lots to drink. Then Sam hurried back home.

Now Sam had everything he needed for his big cookout. Sam could hardly wait to start cooking those juicy burgers. But wait! What burgers?! Sam forgot those too!

Do you know what Sam did next? That's right. Sam went back to the store!

While buying the burgers, Sam saw ice cream. Sam loved ice cream. So Sam bought ice cream too. Then Sam ran back home. Time to get this cookout started!

Great! Now Sam had everything. Sam was finally ready. But wait! There was *one* more thing Sam forgot... Sam forgot to invite his friends!

Now it was too late. All the burgers were done! What could Sam do?

There was only one thing Sam could do. Sam had to eat all those burgers—and all that other food—all by himself!

And that is just what Sam did. Sam ate the burgers, the potato chips, the cookies, the bananas, the candy and the ice cream, too.

Sam enjoyed his big cookout very much.
"I would say this cookout was a grand success," thought Sam.

In fact, Sam thought his big cookout was such a grand success that he decided to do it all over again... *next* Saturday.

## In this Story...

Sam plans a big cookout on the fourth of July. Burgers are Sam's favorite food. But Sam forgets some things he needs, so he goes back to the store. It ends with a surprise, but Sam is happy with his big cookout!

## More Sam Adventures...

Enjoy these other favorites:

- Sam Bakes a Cake
- Sam Visits the Zoo
- Sam Makes a Time Machine
- Sam in Doggie Dreamland
- Sam Needs a Bath
- Sam Makes New Friends
- Sam Finds a Dinosaur Bone!

Visit MrChickenBiscuits.com for a complete list—and have fun!

**Sam the Dog**
Book Series

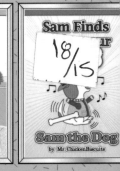

## MrChickenBiscuits.com

ISBN 9781790482917

90000

9 781790 482917

# THE HIDDEN WORLD OF MICROORGANISMS

A HIGH SCHOOL STUDENT'S GUIDE TO MICROBIOLOGY

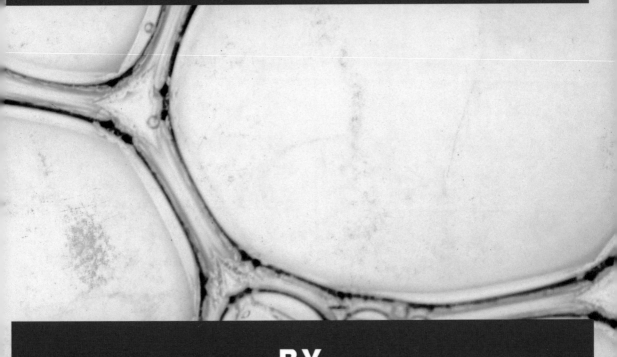

## BY
## DR. ANJANA J.C &  SANATH NAIR